Tonia's Rain Forest

To the Indigenous people of the Amazon and to Ruth Buendía

First edition 2021

Library of Congress Catalog Card Number pending
ISBN 978-1-5362-0845-0

TLF 25 24 23 22 21 20
10 9 8 7 6 5 4 3 2 1

Printed in Dongguan, Guangdong, China

This book was typeset in Garden Essential.
The illustrations were created with acrylic, colored pencil, pastel,
ink, and linocuts and woodcuts on handmade banana bark paper.

Candlewick Press
99 Dover Street
Somerville, Massachusetts 02144

www.candlewick.com

Zonia's Rain Forest

Juana Martinez-Neal

CANDLEWICK PRESS

Zonia lives with those she loves in the rain forest,
where it is always green and full of life.

Every morning, the rain forest calls to Zonia.

Every morning, Zonia answers.

In Zonia's rain forest, green and full of life,
she visits old friends and meets new ones.

"Good morning!" she says one, two, three, four times.

She stops to talk with some chatty new neighbors.

"Welcome! I live next door," Zonia sings.

She says hello to her most playful friend.

"You are my favorite," Zonia whispers.

If she is lucky, her fastest friend will invite her for a short ride through the thicket.

"We are mighty!" Zonia says, for that is what she feels in her heart.

Zonia sees a colorful couple swim by.

"How's the water today?" she asks with a smile.

She congratulates mamas with their new babies.

"I can't wait for you to meet my baby brother.
I love him so much."

Zonia loves playing hide-and-seek.

"Five, six, seven, eight . . ." she counts.

Some friends help Zonia see the world in new ways.

And Zonia knows just who to visit when she
wants to be quiet and still.

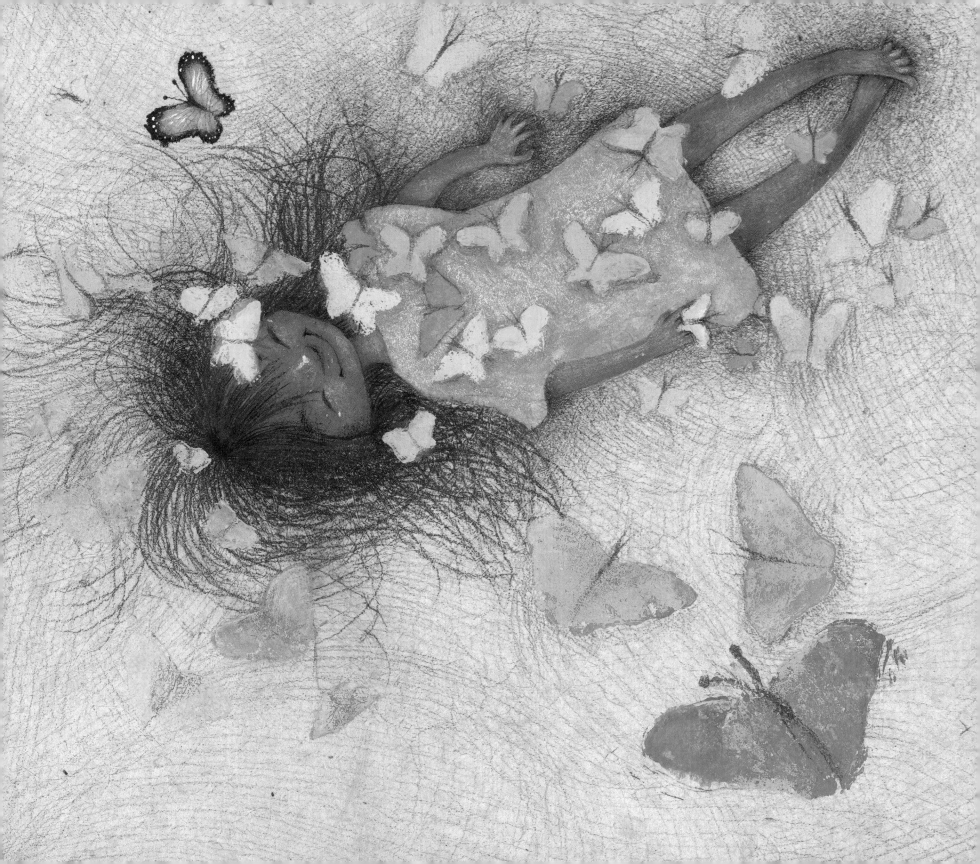

After visiting all of her friends, Zonia is ready to go home.

She can't wait to see her mama and baby brother again.

On her way home, Zonia comes across
something she has not seen before.

Frightened, she runs the rest of the way home.

"Mama, look!" Zonia says, and opens her hands.
"The forest needs help!"

"It is speaking to you," says Zonia's mama.

"Then I will answer," says Zonia, "as I always do.

"We all must answer."

❋ Antamishite Zonia ❋

Zonia osaiki okaratiri maroni añatsiri antamishiki, okantara kenashijenka osheki añantarori. Kitaiterikepe, antamimashi okajemapintiro Zonia. Kitaiterikepe, Zonia akapintiro.

Antamishiteki Zonia okantara kenashijenka osheki saikantarori, okiibántiri peesatiri otsipabintsare aisati obakerari apatyane.
—¡Kitaiteri! —obetsatantapinta aparo, apite, mabaa, otsi apipinitiro.

Ora meka osaikashitiri okinkitsatakayiri obakeraripe aisati kenketsariantipe otsipanampijetari.
—¡Pimpokabejeite! Nosabiki notsipanampijeitami —Zonia okantiri opamposhirianentiri.

Ora obetsatari otsipabintsare ñatsaperotinkari.
—Abirotake nokashiyapintari —Zonia okanttatsatiri.

Aririka okantake, otsipabintsare shintsikiiri ikantero tsamebe aniibetakite tomirishiki.
—¡Arojeipero! —okanti Zonia, irotake okeemiri asankaneki.

Zonia oñake yamatajeiti aparoni tsipatachari ikimoshiretake.
—¿Jaokari okantari nija meeka? —osampijeitakeri oshirontashiriaka.

Ora obeshiriakajeitaro inapee otsipajeitarira entsitepe.
—Nokobaitake iyotitenari obakerari nojaririjaniki. Nonintasanotiri.

Ora Zonia onebetaro oñatsataro otsitibetya.
—Koni, iko, tson, soti… —oñanati ñakarontsipe.

Aparopeni otsipabintsare Zonia yamitakotiro yamenajeitiro kipatsi ora nashyetachari kinkitsashiriantsi. Meka Zonia oyoperoti janika okibaánteri okobi osaike omajerete aisati otekatsite.

Iro meka otsonkakearika okibantiri maaroni otsipabintsare, Zonia betsikaja opiyaje obankoki. Osheki okantimoitajaro oñapajero oniro aisati ojaririjaniki.

Oejatajero awotsiki jatatsiri obankoki, Zonia oñaake kari oñapinte perani. Otsarobashireanake, oshiyaitanaja irosati obankoki.

—¡Inaa, pamene! —okaimapake Zonia ashitariro akope—. ¡Antamimashi okoy amitakotantsi!

—Oñanatatimi —okanti oniro Zonia.

—Iroñaka ari nakakero —akakero Zonia— nokemitapintiro nakiro.

—Marojeini otimatye akajeintero.

Translation of *Zonia's Rain Forest* to Asháninka by Arlynder Sett Gaspar Paulino, translator and interpreter recognized by Peru's Ministry of Culture. For translation to Asháninka variant Satipo-Junín, visit juanamartinezneal.com/zonia.

❋ The Asháninka People ❋

Zonia is Asháninka, which is the largest Indigenous group living in the Peruvian Amazon, with a population estimated at more than 73,000. Their homeland covers a vast region of the Amazon River basin, with the greatest concentration in Peru and in five small, distinct areas of Brazil. Their language, Asháninka, is the most widely used in the Peruvian Amazon.

The Asháninka have a long history of being disenfranchised and forced from their homelands. They have just as long a history of insisting on self-determination. Today, much like Zonia, they are answering the call to protect the rain forest—their home—through activism, community organization, and legal action. Sadly, their rights continue to be ignored and violated, and harassment grows because of others' impatience to develop, cultivate, and mine the world's tropical forests for profit.

At times, the Asháninka use plant-based paint on their faces or bodies to complement their actions or abilities. Varying from family to family, the designs are understood as being empowering and are sometimes inspired by the markings of animals to reflect their attributes. As she may have learned from her mama, Zonia uses red paint made from achiote on the last page of the story to signal strength and determination.

❋ A Few Facts about the Amazon ❋

The Amazon rain forest is home to between four hundred and five hundred different Indigenous groups—some of which are isolated or uncontacted. It is estimated that 330 different languages are spoken among these various groups.

The Amazon rain forest occupies nine different countries: Brazil, Bolivia, Peru, Ecuador, Colombia, Venezuela, Guyana, Suriname, and French Guiana. It covers 1.4 billion acres (567 million hectares), which is about 40 percent of South America. It has 4,100 miles (6,600 kilometers) of rivers, contains half of the earth's remaining forests, and is home to one in ten of the world's known species.

The Amazon rain forest takes carbon dioxide out of the air and turns it into oxygen, producing more than 20 percent of the oxygen on our planet while it helps stabilize climates locally and globally. At the same time, the Amazon rain forest shrinks by 18.7 million acres (7.6 million hectares) every year, or the size of twenty-seven soccer fields every minute. It shrank 17 percent in the last fifty years alone.

❋ Threats to the Amazon ❋

Human collectors of flora and fauna, along with shrinking and breaking up of habitat due to deforestation and illegal mining and logging, are major threats to the survival of the animals and ecosystems in the Amazon rain forest. Every day, the Amazon rain forest is being changed by development. Large infrastructure projects (dams, roads, hydroelectric power plants) and extractive industries (oil wells, mining) have transformed the landscape and the lives of the people who live there, sometimes permanently and not always in positive ways.

❧ ILLEGAL LOGGING

Even in regions where logging or the logging of certain species is illegal, large-scale logging operations still take place. The prized mahogany tree, for example, has been harvested so severely that it is in danger of disappearing altogether.

❧ FARMING

Forests are being burned down and cleared to make room for pastureland on which to graze commercial livestock. Destroying the rain forest also destroys a key source of oxygen (which all living things need in order to keep on living).

❧ MINING

While illegal gold mining is done on a small scale, its effects are anything but small. Illegal mining causes an increase in other types of crime. And, to find even trace amounts of gold, mercury is dumped into the rivers and streams, poisoning the water and all that lives in or depends upon it.

❧ OIL AND GAS EXTRACTION

Oil and gas exploration and extraction take place largely in Indigenous territories. Due to poor environmental practices by these industries, the ability of the people and the land to recover from such damage is severely diminished.

❋ Zonia's Friends (in order of appearance) ❋

Blue morpho butterfly
(Morpho peleides)

Hoffman's two-toed sloth
(Choloepus hoffmanni)

Andean cock-of-the-rock
(Rupicola peruviana)

South American coati
(Nasua nasua)

Jaguar
(Panthera onca)

Amazon river dolphin
(Inia geoffrensis)

Giant anteater
(Myrmecophaga tridactyla)

Spectacled caiman
(Caiman crocodilus)

Giant Amazon water lily
(Victoria amazonica)

Red-tailed boa constrictor
(Boa constrictor)

Arrau turtle
(Podocnemis expansa)

❋ Selected Sources and Resources ❋

www.gob.pe/cultura • www.aidesep.org.pe • www.worldwildlife.org • www.nrdc.org • www.rainforest-alliance.org
For links to these resources and more, visit www.juanamartinezneal.com/zonia.

"The peoples concerned shall have the right to decide their own priorities for the process of development as it affects their lives, beliefs, institutions and spiritual well-being and the lands they occupy or otherwise use, and to exercise control, to the extent possible, over their own economic, social and cultural development. In addition, they shall participate in the formulation, implementation and evaluation of plans and programmes for national and regional development which may affect them directly."

UN ILO Indigenous and Tribal Peoples Convention, No. 169 (1989)
Copyright © International Labour Organization 2020

❋ ❋ ❋

ACKNOWLEDGMENTS: Many thanks to the team at Salud Sin Límites Peru (www.saludsinlimitesperu.org.pe): Gerardo Seminario Namuch, Leonardo Cortéz Farfán, and Yely Palomino Flores. Thanks to Julián and Lucila Flores, Javier Huaja Estrada, Central Asháninka del Río Tambo (CART) and the Comunidad Nativa de Betania, Fenicia Inca, Armando Perez, Herminia Juan Samuel, Luzibeth Juan Perez, Reúnen Roman and Mady Vargas, Monica Macedo Gonzalez, Hioner Guimaraes Pinedo, Tita Lucia, Tita Ana, Tita Celia, Cassius Clay Torres, Margarita Vasquez, and Clay Smith Torres Vasquez. Thanks to Arlynder Sett Gaspar Paulino and Deniz Contreras Alva for their translations of the manuscript to Asháninka, and to Edgar Shamayre Bantico, Miqueas Sanchoma Morales, Abelina Ampinti Shiñungari, and Abelardo Rodríguez Pishirovanti for vetting the Asháninka Satipo-Junin translation for fidelity and accuracy. My profound thanks to Ruth Buendía and Luisa Elvira Belaunde for their immense knowledge. Thanks to the women paper artisans of Chazuta who hand-made the paper used to paint the illustrations in this book. Thanks to Rocío Molina Paredes, Emilio, Rafaela, and the Molina Paredes family. Thanks to Marilú Ponte, Molly Idle, Stefanie Sánchez Von Borstel, Mary Lee Donovan, Melanie Cordova, Ann Stott, and the amazing people from Candlewick Press. Gracias. Pasoṅki. Aronega. Irake. Thank you.